TALES OF AMANDA PIG

Jean Van Leeuwen

PICTURES BY

ANN SCHWENINGER

DIAL BOOKS FOR YOUNG READERS

E. P. Dutton, Inc. NEW YORK

Dial easy-to-read

Published by
Dial Books for Young Readers
A Division of E. P. Dutton, Inc.
2 Park Avenue
New York, New York 10016

The Dial Easy-to-Read logo is a trademark of
Dial Books for Young Readers
a division of E. P. Dutton, Inc., ® TM 1,162,718

Library of Congress Cataloging in Publication Data
Van Leeuwen, Jean. Tales of Amanda Pig.
Summary: Amanda Pig, her brother Oliver, and their
parents share a busy day, working and playing together
from breakfast to bedtime.
[1. Pigs—Fiction. 2. Family life—Fiction]
I. Schweninger, Ann, ill. II. Title.
PZ7.V3273Tak 1983 [E] 82-23545
ISBN 0-8037-8443-0 ISBN-8037-8450-3 (lib. bdg.)

First Edition
10 9 8 7 6 5 4 3 2 1

The art for each picture consists of a pencil and wash drawing
with two halftone color separations.

Reading Level 1.8

For Elizabeth,
this one is just for you.

J.V.L.

To Pat Roche

A.S.

CONTENTS

AMANDA'S EGG

Father and Mother

and Oliver and Amanda

sat at the table eating breakfast.

Father took his last bite of egg.

"I am going outside

to rake leaves," he said.

"Will you excuse me?"

"Yes," said Mother.

"Eat your egg, Amanda."

Amanda looked at her egg.

It looked back at her

with its funny yellow eye.

She didn't eat it.

Oliver took his last bite of toast.

"May I go outside too?" he asked.

"Yes," said Mother.

"Eat your egg, Amanda."

Amanda looked at her egg.

If she touched it with her fork,

it would wiggle.

She didn't eat it.

Mother took her last sip of tea.
"I am going to wash the dishes,"
she said. "Eat your egg, Amanda."
Amanda looked at her egg.
The yellow part would run out
all over her nice clean toast.
She didn't eat it.

Mother washed all the dishes.

"Amanda," she said.

"You still haven't eaten your egg."

"It is cold," said Amanda.

"It is cold because
you didn't eat it," said Mother.

"Eggs are good for you, Amanda.

Eggs make you big and strong."

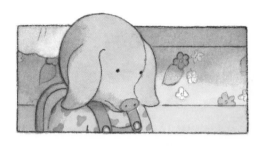

Amanda looked at her egg.

It felt funny going down too,

not like real food, but slippery.

She didn't eat it.

"I will close my eyes

and count to ten," said Mother.

"When I open my eyes,

your egg will be gone."

Mother closed her eyes.

"One, two, three, four, five,

six, seven, eight, nine, ten."

Mother opened her eyes.

Amanda's egg was still there.

Mother sat at the table

looking out the window.

Amanda sat at the table

looking at her egg.

"Oh, there's Father," said Mother.

"He is raking leaves.

And Oliver is helping him."

Amanda looked at her egg.
"They are raking the leaves
into a big pile," said Mother.

"Now they are jumping into the pile
and covering each other
with leaves."

"I'm all done," said Amanda.

"What?" said Mother.

"Look at my plate," said Amanda.

"I don't see your egg," said Mother.

"Did you throw it on the floor?"

"No," said Amanda.

"Did you put it in your pocket?"

"No," said Amanda.

"Then you must have thrown it out the window for the birds to eat."

"No," said Amanda. "I ate it."

"You wouldn't do that," said Mother.

"I did," said Amanda.

"May I go outside now?"

"Yes," said Mother.

THE VERY LONG TRIP

"What can we do on a rainy day?" asked Amanda.

"You could do puzzles," said Mother.

"All the puzzles

have pieces missing," said Oliver.

"Amanda ate them

when she was a baby."

"You could read books," said Mother.

"I've read them all," said Amanda.

"Let's go to Grandmother's house."

"Not today," said Mother.

"It is a long trip

and it is raining too hard."

"We could take you in our airplane,"
said Oliver.

"In that case," said Mother,

"I would be happy to go."

Oliver and Amanda got the airplane
ready for takeoff.

Mother climbed into the backseat.

"Hold on," said Oliver.

"We're taking off."

There was a loud noise.

"What was that?" asked Mother.

"The engine," said Oliver.

"I think something is broken."

He took his screwdriver

and lay down next to the airplane.

"It's fixed now," he said.

The airplane flew for a few minutes.

"Lunchtime!" said Amanda.

She climbed out of the airplane.

"You can't get out," said Oliver.

"We are flying in the air."

"Oh," said Amanda.

She climbed back in.

Oliver landed the airplane.

"Let's sit in the grass

and have a picnic," said Amanda.

"What are we having?" asked Mother.

"Chocolate chip sandwiches,"

said Amanda.

"And raisins for dessert."

They had their picnic.

"Now it's my turn to be the driver," said Amanda.

The airplane flew some more.

"Are we almost there?" asked Mother.

"Yes," said Amanda.

There was a terrible noise.

"What was that?" asked Mother.

"We landed on Grandmother's roof," said Amanda.

"But we didn't break it."

"Hello, Grandmother," said Oliver.

"Well, we have to go now. Good-bye."

"That was a short visit,"

said Mother.

"We can't stay all night,"

said Amanda.

"We forgot our toothbrushes."

They flew home.

"Look," said Mother.

"The rain has stopped."

Oliver and Amanda looked outside.

There was Grandmother

coming up the front walk.

"Grandmother!" said Amanda.
"We wanted to visit you
but it was raining too hard.
So we flew to your house
in our airplane."

"I wanted to visit you too,"
said Grandmother. "And here I am."
"It was a very long trip,"
said Oliver.
"Yes, it was," said Grandmother.
"But I'm glad I came."
"Me too," said Amanda.

THE MONSTER

"I can't go upstairs," said Amanda.

"There is a monster in the hall."

"That's dumb," said Oliver.

"Monsters are just pretend, Amanda," said Mother.

"Not this one," said Amanda.

"Show it to me," said Father.

Amanda pointed up the stairs.

"Hmm," said Father.

"I always thought that was a clock."

"It is in the daytime," said Amanda.

"At night it is a monster."

"I see what you mean," said Father.

"There are its eyes."

"And its mouth," said Amanda.

"And it has funny wings too."

"I don't think I want
to go upstairs either," said Father.

"Oh, Father," said Amanda.

"Grown-ups aren't scared of monsters."

"Not usually," said Father.

"But this one is pretty scary."

"What can we do?" asked Amanda.

"Hmm," said Father.

"I have an idea."

He got his flashlight

and a cooking pot

and two Halloween masks

and his umbrella.

"Here is the plan," he said.

"We will put on these masks.

Then we will stamp upstairs.

You will bang on the pot

and I will shine my flashlight

in the monster's eyes.

We are going to scare that monster."

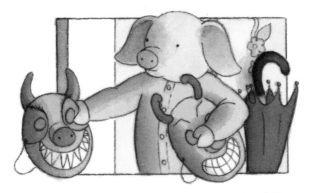

"What is the umbrella for?"

asked Amanda.

"Just in case," said Father.

Father and Amanda got ready.

"Watch out, Monster!" called Father.

"We are coming up!"

Father and Amanda stamped upstairs.

Amanda banged on the pot.

Father shone his flashlight
in the monster's eyes.

They stamped all the way
down the hall to Amanda's room.
"Well, I guess we took care of
that monster," said Father.

"Father," said Amanda.

"When you were shining the light

in the monster's eyes,

it didn't look like a monster.

It looked like a clock."

"Really?" said Father.

"Then maybe there is no monster?"

"Maybe," said Amanda.

Father shone his flashlight

at the monster again.

"See?" said Amanda.

"That's a relief," said Father.

"Now we can go to bed."

Father tucked Amanda in.

"Father," said Amanda. "What if
I have to get up in the night
and it is very dark
and the clock looks
like a monster again?"

"Hmm," said Father. "I know what.
I will leave the masks
and the pot and the flashlight
and the umbrella by your bed."
"Just in case?" said Amanda.
"Just in case," said Father.

THE FIGHT

"Let's play house," said Amanda.
"You always want to play house,"
said Oliver. "Let's play monsters."

"How do you do that?"

asked Amanda.

"Simple," said Oliver.

"You are you and I am the monster

and I come to eat you up."

"No," said Amanda.

"Amanda's afraid of monsters,"

said Oliver.

"I am not," said Amanda.

"Then let's play," said Oliver.

"I am the terrible Booba-Monster.

I see a nice fat baby.

The Booba-Monster likes to eat

nice fat babies."

"I'm not playing," said Amanda.

"And I'm not a fat baby.

If you think so,

you can get out of my room."

"You can't make me," said Oliver.
"The Booba-Monster does
what he wants."
"Father," said Amanda,
"Oliver is bothering me."
"Amanda is bothering me,"
said Oliver.

"Maybe you should play
by yourselves for a little while,"
said Father.

"Mean dumb Oliver," said Amanda.
"Go away. And never come back!"

"Fat baby Amanda," said Oliver.
"Don't worry. I won't!"

He slammed the door.

"Ah, peace and quiet," said Amanda.
She sat her rabbit and her monkey
at her little table.

"I am the mother," she said,
"and you are the babies.
Come on, Rabbit. Eat your egg.
Eggs make you big and strong.
No, I don't know when
Father will be home."

Amanda went to the living room.

"I have nothing to do," she said.

"I thought you were playing house,"
said Father.

"It's no fun alone," said Amanda.

"I have nothing to do either,"
said Oliver.

"Maybe you can play together now,"
said Father.

"Come to my room," said Amanda.
"The babies are waiting
for the father to come home."

"I still don't want to play house,"
said Oliver.
"How about Monster House?"
said Amanda.
"I'll be the mother monster
and you can be the father monster."
"Well," said Oliver. "Okay."

"Come on, Father Monster,"
said Amanda.

"Where are we going,
Mother Monster?" asked Oliver.

"I know where there are some
nice fat babies," said Amanda.

"Let's go eat them up."

SLEEPING TIME

"Good night, Amanda," said Mother.

"Good night, Mother," said Amanda.

"I am not sleepy."

"You're not?" said Mother.

"I am very sleepy."

"I know what," said Amanda.

"You be the little girl

and I'll be the mother

and I will put you to bed."

"That would be nice," said Mother.

Amanda got out of bed

and Mother got in.

Amanda pulled the quilt up.

"Now you are nice and cozy,"

she said. "Would you like a story?"

"Yes, please," said Mother.

"'Once there was a princess, and

she lived with her mother and father

in a big, big castle.'

And that's the end of the story,"

said Amanda. "How about a song?"

"Yes, please," said Mother.

"'When you are asleep in your bed
and you hear a strange noise
it might be an owl, or it might not
but don't worry, I am here.'

And that's the end of the song,"
said Amanda.

"Now it's time to go to sleep."

Amanda tucked Mother in.

She gave Mother her rabbit to hug

and kissed her good night.

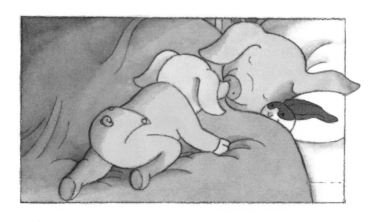

"Good night, sweet potato," she said.

Mother did not answer.

Her eyes were closed.

"I think my little girl

is asleep," said Amanda.

Amanda sat

and watched Mother sleep.

It seemed very quiet in the room.

And empty.

And a little bit cold.

Amanda touched Mother.

"Wake up," she said.

Mother kept on sleeping.

"It's my turn," said Amanda, louder.

She took off Mother's quilt.

"Whoo hah, what?" Mother snorted.

She sat up.

"I said it's my turn," said Amanda.

"But I'm nice and cozy,"

said Mother.

"You be the mother now,"
said Amanda.

"And I'll be the little girl."

"Well, all right," said Mother.

She got out of bed

and Amanda got in.

"Now it's time to go to sleep,"
said Mother.

She tucked Amanda in.

She gave Amanda her rabbit to hug
and kissed her good night.

"Good night, sweet potato,"
said Mother.

"Good night, Mother," said Amanda.